Treble Recorder
Sight-reading
from 2018

ABRSM Grades 1–5

Contents

First published in 2017 by ABRSM (Publishing) Ltd, a wholly owned subsidiary of ABRSM
© 2017 by The Associated Board of the Royal Schools of Music
Unauthorized photocopying is illegal

Music origination by Moira Roach
Cover by Kate Benjamin & Andy Potts
Printed in England by Page Bros (Norwich) Ltd, on materials from sustainable sources

Grade 1

Grade 1

6

Grade 2

Grade 2

Grade 2

Grade 3

Grade 3

Grade 3

Grade 4

Grade 4

Grade 4

Grade 4

Grade 5

Grade 5

7

8

9

Grade 5

13 **Amabile**

14 **Scherzando**

15 **Allegretto scherzando**

Grade 5

19

Andante sostenuto

20

Vivo

21

Marziale

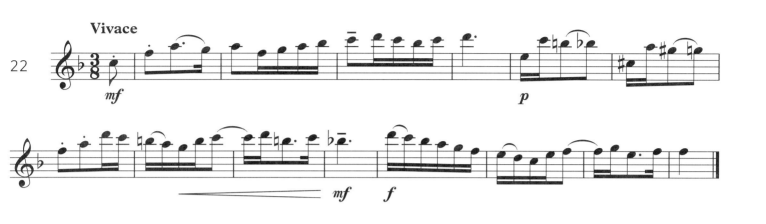